Postman Pat
and the
Pet Show

Story by John Cunliffe
Pictures by Joan Hickson

From the original Television designs by Ivor Wood

André Deutsch/Hippo Books

Scholastic Children's Books,
Scholastic Publications Ltd,
7-9 Pratt Street, London NW1 0AE, UK

Scholastic Inc.,
730 Broadway, New York, NY 10003, USA

Scholastic Canada Ltd,
123 Newkirk Road, Richmond Hill,
Ontario, Canada L4C 3G5

Ashton Scholastic Pty Ltd,
PO Box 579, Gosford, New South Wales,
Australia

Ashton Scholastic Ltd,
Private Bag 1, Penrose, Auckland,
New Zealand

First published by André Deutsch Ltd, 1988
Text copyright © 1988 John Cunliffe
Illustrations copyright © 1988 by André Deutsch Limited
Scholastic Publications Limited and
Woodland Animations Limited

ISBN: 0 233 98296 5 (hardback)
ISBN: 0 590 70976 3 (paperback)

Made and printed in Belgium by Proost

10 9 8 7 6 5 4

There was a new poster in Greendale
Post Office.

"That'll be a good day if it's fine," said Pat. "I wonder if Miss Hubbard will be selling some of her nettle wine? I mustn't miss that."

"Never mind the wine," said Mrs. Goggins. "Aren't you going in for the pet show? It's a lot more fun if you show something."

"Well, I don't know," said Pat. "I suppose we could show Julian's white mice, but the Reverend doesn't like mice. He'd run a mile if he saw them."

"No, you don't want to be showing mice," said Mrs. Goggins. "Why don't you show Jess? He's a lovely cat. He's sure to win a prize."

"Mmm," said Pat, "not a bad idea. Perhaps I will. Mind you, I don't know what Jess will think of being in a show."

When Pat told Sara, the first thing she said was, "If that cat's going in for the pet show, he'll need a bath, and a good brushing. Just look at him!"

Jess had been after mice in the Pottages' barn. He looked very dusty, and he had pieces of straw in his fur.

"Jess doesn't like going in the bath," said Julian.

"Just like somebody else in this house," said Sara. "But he'll have to go in the bath just the same, show or no show. I don't think he's had a bath since he was stuck up that tree."

After tea, Pat got the old baby bath
out, and put it on the kitchen table.
Then he began to fill it with buckets of
warm water.

Sara found a bottle of shampoo.

When Jess saw what was going on,

he went and hid behind the sofa.

He knew the baby bath was for him.

Oh dear! Jess hated having a bath. He didn't like water. He didn't like soap. He didn't like shampoo. He could wash himself with his tongue, and that, he thought, was good enough for any cat. But Sara found Jess behind the sofa, and brought him to the kitchen, with all his claws out, and put him in the bath.

What a splashing he made!

It was like bathing ten cats all at once.

"If only you'd keep still, Jess, the soap wouldn't go in your eyes!" said Pat. But Jess would not keep still. Jess could not keep still.

And the soap, and the water,

and the shampoo went in his eyes,

and all over the table and the floor,

and over Pat, and Sara, and Julian.

In the end, when Pat had mopped
the floor, they all had to have a bath.

And then, when they were all dry again, Jess had to be brushed and combed. He didn't like this, either. This was Sara's job, and she was as gentle as she knew how to be.

But Jess's fur was so tangled with going through hedges forwards and backwards and sideways, and creeping in ditches, and hunting for mice in the hay, that the comb pulled and tugged at him, and hurt him. Poor Jess. He didn't know why he had to be so clean and tidy. When all the brushing and combing was finished, Jess looked lovely. He looked like one of the cats advertising cat food on television.

"You're a real beauty, now, Jess," said Sara. "You're sure to win the first prize at the show."

The next day, Pat called on Miss
Hubbard with a parcel, and she said,
"Have you got a new cat? Where has
Jess gone?"
"It is Jess," said Pat, laughing. "He's
just clean for once."

And he told Miss Hubbard all about
Jess's bath, and the Show.
"I have just the thing," she said. She
took a yellow silk ribbon from her
sewing-box. "Look! Isn't it pretty?"
She tied it in a bow round Jess's neck.

Jess hated that bow. It tickled him,
and he felt so silly in a yellow silk bow.
He shook it. He bit it. He scratched it.

In the end it fell off. When Pat found it, it was too dusty and dirty to put on again.

And then, what do you think Jess did, the day before the Show? He went hunting rabbits somewhere the other side of the little wood. That meant going through quite a few hedges and muddy ditches, and he came back looking as though he had never had a bath at all.

"Dear me, Jess," said Pat, "you can't go to the Show like that."

But when Jess saw Pat getting the baby bath out again, he was off through the open door before Sara could shut it. He didn't come back for his supper, and he found a warm place in the Pottages' barn to sleep.

The next day was Show Day. There was no sign of Jess, so they had to go to the pet show without him.

"I don't think Jess wanted to come to the Show, anyway," said Julian.

At Ted Glen's coconut shy, Pat won a big food hamper.

Sara bought a woolly jumper at
Granny Dryden's knitting stall.

Julian bought a chocolate cake at Mrs Thompson's cake stall.

Alf Thompson's dog, Towser, won the
pet show.

"Where is Jess?" they all asked.

"I think he's decided he isn't a show-
cat," said Pat.

They had a lovely time at the show.
Jess had a lovely time, too, sunbathing
on the roof of Alf's pigsty. But he was
waiting by the back door when Pat,
and Sara, and Julian came home.
Jess decided to stay at home when he
was *sure* that no one was going to get
the baby bath out.

When Pat opened the food hamper, he found a big tin of sardines in it.

"Here's a prize for you, Jess," said Pat, "even though you didn't come to the show."

And Jess ate them for his supper.